Billie B. Brown

Billie B. Brown Books

The Bad Butterfly
The Soccer Star
The Midnight Feast
The Second-best Friend
The Extra-special Helper
The Beautiful Haircut
The Big Sister
The Spotty Vacation
The Birthday Mix-up
The Secret Message
The Little Lie
The Best Project
The Deep End
The Copycat Kid
The Night Fright

First American Edition 2013
Kane Miller, A Division of EDC Publishing

Text copyright © 2010 Sally Rippin
Illustrations copyright © 2010 Aki Fukuoka
Logo and design copyright © 2010 Hardie Grant Egmont

First published in Australia in 2010 by Hardie Grant Egmont

For information contact:
Kane Miller, A Division of EDC Publishing
P.O. Box 470663
Tulsa, OK 74147-0663
www.kanemiller.com
www.edcpub.com
www.usbornebooksandmore.com

Library of Congress Control Number: 2011935697

Printed and bound in the United States of America
12 13 14 15 16 17 18
ISBN: 978-1-61067-099-9

The
Extra-special
Helper

By Sally Rippin

Illustrated by Aki Fukuoka

Kane Miller
A DIVISION OF EDC PUBLISHING

Chapter One

Billie B. Brown has one sun hat, one water bottle and fourteen clipboards. Do you want to know what the "B" in Billie B. Brown stands for?

Bossy.

Billie B. Brown can sometimes be just a teensy bit bossy. Like today, for example. Billie and her class are going on a field trip. They are going to the zoo.

Do you know why Billie is carrying so many clipboards?

Fourteen clipboards

Sun hat

Water bottle

Ms. Walton has asked Billie to be her extra-special helper.

Billie is helping Ms. Walton carry all the clipboards for their field trip. Usually Ella and Tracey get to be Ms. Walton's helpers, but today Ms. Walton has chosen Billie.

Billie feels very **proud**.
She gets to sit next to
Ms. Walton on the bus.

"You will have to help me make sure nobody gets lost today, Billie," Ms. Walton says. "It's a very important job."

"Of course," says Billie.

"OK, now, not so much noise, please!" Ms. Walton calls out to the boys at the back of the bus.

6

Billie turns around to look.

The boys at the back are
making a lot of **noise**.

Billie waves to Jack.

Jack is Billie's best friend.

They have been
best friends since they
were babies.

Usually Billie and Jack
sit together.

But today Billie is being Ms. Walton's extra-special helper, so Jack is sitting with the other boys at the back of the bus.

The boys are laughing, and Sam is singing a loud song.

"Billie," Ms. Walton says, "can you please go and ask the boys to keep it down a bit?"

Billie walks to the back
of the bus.

"You boys are making
too much noise!" she says.

"Who says?" asks Sam.

"Yeah, who says?" asks Benny.

Benny is Sam's best friend.

"Ms. Walton," says Billie. "She told me to tell you to keep it down."

Benny looks at Jack. Sam looks at Jack.

Jack shrugs. "Sorry, Billie," he says. "We'll try to be quieter."

"Good!" says Billie, and she marches back to the front of the bus.

"Thank you, Billie," Ms. Walton says.

Billie beams. She likes being an extra-special helper.

Chapter Two

When they get to the
zoo, Ms. Walton tells the
class to form two lines.
One line is in front of
Ms. Walton, and the other
line is in front of Billie.

Ms. Walton and Billie hand out the clipboards.

"Now, hold on to your clipboards, please," says Ms. Walton. "I want them all back at the end of the day."

"Don't lose the clipboards," Billie says, handing them out to Benny, Sam and Jack.

Jack frowns. "I won't!"
he says.

"I'm just saying, that's
all," says Billie, walking
down the line.

"Now, everyone stay together," Ms. Walton says. "I don't want to lose anyone, OK?"

"**OK**!" everyone in Billie's class shouts.

They are all very **excited**. A day at the zoo is much more fun than school!

"Great!" says Ms. Walton.

"First we are going to look at the reptiles. I want you to put the animals you see today into two groups: warmblooded and coldblooded, OK?"

Benny puts up his hand. "What's warmblooded and coldblooded?"

Ms. Walton sighs. "Benny,
we have been learning
about this all year!"

"Don't worry, Ms. Walton,"
Billie says. "I'll help Benny."

Benny frowns. "No, thanks,"
he says. "You are already
helping Ms. Walton.
Jack can help me."

"Sure!" says Jack.

Jack swings his arm over Benny's shoulder. "It's easy. Look."

Billie watches Benny and Jack talking together. She feels a teensy bit **jealous**.

Usually Jack is her partner in class. But then Ms. Walton asks Billie to help her hand out pencils, and Billie feels important again.

"Billie, I need you to walk at the end of the line to make sure no one gets left behind," says Ms. Walton.

Billie scrunches up her forehead. She doesn't want to walk at the end of the line. She wants to walk in the middle of the line with Jack. Or up at the front with Ms. Walton.

But Ms. Walton has asked Billie to be her extra-special helper today, so Billie nods.

"Um, OK," says Billie.

"Thank you," says
Ms. Walton. "It's very
important that no one
gets lost. The zoo is a
very big place!"

Chapter Three

The class walks in two lines to the reptile house. Billie walks at the end of the two lines to make sure nobody gets lost. She has a very important job to do!

They look at the lizards and tortoises and crocodiles. Billie knows that these animals are all coldblooded. They have studied this in class. She writes them down on her list.

Next, they go to
look at the monkeys.
The monkeys are Billie's
favorite. Billie especially
loves the baby chimpanzees.
They are so cheeky!
Billie puts monkeys
under the warmblooded
heading. Too easy!

Billie looks up from
her clipboard.

Sam, Benny and Jack
are making silly faces
at the
monkeys.
Billie thinks
they look
very funny.
They
look like
monkeys themselves!
She giggles.

But then Ms. Walton looks
over. "Come on, boys!" she
calls. "You're holding up
the line!"

Billie marches over
to the boys. She had
almost forgotten her
important job. She has
to make sure no one gets
left behind!

"Hurry up!" she says.
"Come on! Everyone's
waiting!"

"You are very bossy
today, Billie!" says Jack.

Billie looks at Jack.
He is not making a silly
monkey face anymore.
He is not even making
a happy Jack face.

He is making a very
cross face. And he is
making that cross face
at Billie!

Billie feels all **jumbled up**
inside. She wants Jack to
be happy with her.

28

Jack is her best friend.

But she wants Ms. Walton
to be happy with her too.
She is Ms. Walton's
extra-special helper.
Billie doesn't want to let
her down.

Billie frowns. "I'm not
bossy. I just have to make
sure no one gets lost!"
she says.

She walks behind
the boys to the back of
the line. If Jack is **cross**
with her then she is
cross with him too!

The class walks out of
the monkey area and
along the path to their
next stop. They look at
the lions and tigers and
the long-necked giraffes.

Then they walk through the steamy butterfly room.

Billie writes down all the animals on her sheet of paper. She knows all the answers.

Chapter Four

Soon they come to the sea creatures. They go into a dark tunnel under the water.

Billie stands in front of the glass and watches the dolphins.

They duck and weave
and **chatter**. Billie thinks
they are wonderful.

A baby dolphin swims next
to his mother, bobbing
his head up and down.
Billie waves, and the baby
dolphin opens his mouth
into a big smile.

Hmmm, Billie wonders.

*Are dolphins warmblooded
or coldblooded?*

Billie can't
remember.
*Do baby
dolphins come
out of eggs?*
She isn't sure.

Billie has an idea.
She will ask Jack for help.

Every time Billie is
stuck on a question
in class, Jack helps her.
If Jack gets stuck, Billie
helps him. That's what
best friends do.

Billie looks around for Jack.
But Jack is nowhere
to be seen. In fact, the
whole class has gone!
Billie has been left behind!

Billie runs out of
the tunnel. She looks
to the left. Nobody!
She looks to the right.
Nobody! Billie is lost!
She feels like she is going
to cry.

Suddenly, from around
the corner, a face appears.
The face has freckles
and a big goofy smile.
Do you know who it is?

That's right, it's Jack!
He has come back
for Billie. She has never
been so happy to see him.

"Come on, Billie," he jokes.

"You're holding everyone up!"

Billie blushes. "Sorry for being so bossy before," she says. "Thanks for coming back."

"That's OK," says Jack, holding Billie's hand. "I know you were just trying to help Ms. Walton."

"I was so worried about everyone else getting lost that I got lost myself!" says Billie.

"Lucky I noticed that you were gone," says Jack.

Billie feels lucky to
have such a good friend.
Then she has an idea.
"Hey, will you walk at
the back with me?"

"Sure," says Jack, smiling.
Then suddenly, he
frowns. "Oh no!" he says.

"What?" asks Billie.
She is **worried** he may
have changed his mind.

Maybe he doesn't want to walk with her anymore?

"Your clipboard! Where is it?" Jack says.

"Oh, I must have left it near the dolphins!" Billie gasps. "I am not a very good helper today, am I?" she says. "I think I need my own extra-special helper!'

Jack laughs. "Come on. Let's go and get your clipboard before we are *both* lost!" he says.

"You are very bossy today, Jack," says Billie. But she is smiling.

They both run back into the tunnel to find the clipboard.

Then they run as fast as they can to join the end of the line again.

And do you know what? They are so fast that nobody even notices they were gone!